HANNAH MONTANA
THE MOVIE

The Movie Storybook

Based on the screenplay written by Dan Berendsen
Based on characters created by Michael Poryes and Rich Correll & Barry O'Brien
Executive Producers Michael Poryes and Steve Peterman, David Blocker
Produced by Alfred Gough and Miles Millar
Directed by Peter Chelsom

Printed in the United States of America
First Edition
1 3 5 7 9 10 8 6 4 2
Library of Congress Catalog Card Number on file.

For more Disney Press fun, visit www.disneybooks.com
Visit www.disney.com/HannahMontanaMovie

ISBN 978-1-4231-1817-6

DISNEY PRESS
New York

"Hannah! Hannah! Hannah!"

The chants swelled inside the stadium. Thousands of eager fans were waiting for Hannah Montana to take the stage. More were still pouring in from outside. The concert was due to begin any minute.

Outside the stadium, Miley Stewart and her best friend, Lilly Truscott, were pushing their way toward the ticket booth.

Finally, they reached the window. "Please," Miley pleaded. "We've got to get in there!"

"Our names are on the list!" Lilly added.

The ticket clerk rolled her eyes. "In your dreams, Sweet Cheeks," she scoffed. "Next!"

The two girls were swept back into the crowd.

"You're the only pop star I know who can't get into her own concert," Lilly said. Lilly was one of the few people who knew Miley's secret: that she was Hannah Montana.

Miley knew her father must be frantic by now. How was she going to get inside? Just then a security guard drove by in a golf cart. He parked and climbed out. Miley stared at the golf cart. Suddenly, she had an idea.

"Stop those girls!" the guard shouted as the golf cart sputtered into motion.

Miley stomped on the gas pedal and drove into the stadium. They drove up and down the backstage hallways. They all looked exactly the same. Finally, Miley spotted her dad.

Robby Ray Stewart was standing outside the dressing room, a worried look on his face.

"Sorry," Miley said breathlessly. "Practice ran late, and Jackson's car wouldn't start, and—"

"Less explaining, more changing," Mr. Stewart said. "We don't have a lot of time."

Miley nodded. She glanced at the large makeup box by the dressing-room mirror. She called it the Hannah Box. Nobody would ever guess that it held everything needed to transform a regular girl into a superstar.

Before she knew it, Miley was striding down the hallway toward the stage. A long, sleek, blond wig covered her brown hair. She was dressed in a short, shimmery dress and stylish boots.

She was Hannah Montana.

Her father waited with her below the stage. The ceiling above them opened up to reveal the stage and the bright spotlights. The roar of the crowd was deafening.

"Don't forget, it's your turn to do the dishes tonight," Mr. Stewart said as Miley stood on the lift that would bring her up to the stage.

"Oh, come on," Miley replied. "I did them last night."

"You're the one who wanted the best of both worlds!" her father called as she disappeared through the ceiling.

Miley smiled as the crowd cheered her appearance. She loved being on stage in the spotlight as Hannah Montana. She started to sing and the cheers grew even louder. Being a teen pop star was so much fun!

A few days later, Miley was at the beach shooting a Hannah Montana video. Miley was dancing with surfers and posing with a supercute lifeguard as she sang. The surfers even lifted her up on a surfboard and carried her around the beach while she posed!

"Cut!" the director called. "Hannah, as always, fabulous! That's a wrap, people."

Take Care of Tide Pools

Miley headed to her makeshift dressing room, which was a tent set up on the sand. She sat down beside the Hannah Box. As she reached up to take off her wig, she spotted something moving in the clothes rack nearby.

No, not something. Someone.

Miley screamed.

A goofy-looking man with buck teeth and thick glasses stumbled forward.

"I'm sorry!" the man exclaimed. "I just *had* to meet you. I promised my girls I'd say hi for them. Hi!" He pulled out a camera. "Do you mind?"

"Go ahead," Miley said, amused. He was almost as giddy as one of her young fans!

The man lifted the camera. But just as he was about to snap the picture, Vita, Hannah's publicist, barreled into the tent.

"Don't even think about it!" she snapped. Vita glared at the visitor. "Hello, Oswald."

The man took off his glasses and spit out his fake teeth. "Hello, Vita," he said. His voice now had a British accent.

Miley stared in surprise.

Vita turned to Miley and said, "Oswald Granger. Chief sleaze for *Bon Chic*, England's most notorious tabloid." She turned back to Oswald and said, "Now get out!"

Oswald shrugged and left the tent quickly. But neither Miley nor Vita noticed that he left his camera behind—or that the little red "record" button was flashing. He was determined to discover Miley's secret.

Vita turned back to Miley. "He didn't see anything, did he?" she hissed.

"I don't think so," Miley replied.

"Good. Hannah, don't talk to anybody unless I'm by your side. That's why you hired me, remember?"

Vita noticed a notebook lying open on the dressing table. "What's this?" she asked.

"Nothing." Miley shrugged. "Just a song I'm writing."

"On your own? That's sweet," Vita said. "But you have people for that. You need to concentrate on what you do best—singing your scrappy blond heart out. Let me worry about everything else." She glanced at the Hannah Box. "Like making sure your little secret *stays* a secret."

Oswald's plan had worked perfectly . . . *almost*. As soon as Miley and Vita left the tent, he darted back in and grabbed his camera. It had recorded everything! The trouble was, Vita was blocking the picture the whole time.

He called Lucinda, his editor at *Bon Chic*, and tried to explain. "Apparently, there's a secret."

"Find me that secret!" Lucinda ordered. "She's the most popular teenager in the world."

"Tell me about it!" Oswald said. "When my girls heard who I was coming to interview, Daddy suddenly had a real job!"

"Mess this up," Lucinda warned, "and Daddy won't have any job at all!"

A few days later, Miley was back to her regular life. She and Lilly were in gym class planning the final details for Lilly's Sweet Sixteen party that night. "As soon as the bell rings we've got to bolt," Lilly said. "There are a million things left to do for my party!"

Miley nodded. Right after school she had to say good-bye to her brother, Jackson, who was leaving for college in Tennessee. Then she could focus on Lilly's party.

But after gym class, Miley found Vita waiting with big news. Hannah Montana had just been invited to perform at the New York Music Awards!

"That's great!" Miley said. She was ready to burst with excitement. "But what am I going to wear?"

"The car and the Box are out front," Vita replied. "Hannah has to do a major shop—right now."

They rushed toward the door. Just then Lilly came out of the gym.

"Miley?" she called.

"Minor Hannah emergency," Miley called back. "I'll be there. Promise!"

A few hours later, Miley, dressed as Hannah, was loaded down with shopping bags.

"Now wasn't that fun?" Vita said.

"It feels kind of weird having them give me all this stuff for free," Miley admitted.

"You're a star!" Vita smiled. "Name it and it's yours!"

They headed into another fancy department store.

When Miley looked at a display of watches, she cried, "Is that the time? We've got to go!"

She'd forgotten about Jackson leaving for college. And Lilly's birthday party!

Miley raced out of the store and jumped into the limo, followed by Vita. As she was about to yank off her wig, she spotted someone in the car right behind them—the sneaky British reporter, Oswald Granger!

"Step on it!" Vita told the limo driver.

It was too late to say good-bye to Jackson, so the limo headed straight for Lilly's party. But the driver couldn't lose Oswald. Miley didn't dare get out of the car looking like herself. She'd have to show up as Hannah Montana. She just hoped Lilly would understand. . . .

Lilly's party was in full swing. Hundreds of people were eating, dancing to a live band, and trying out the skateboard ramp. Lilly was showing off some of her best skater moves.

Just then, she heard a guy ask, "Hey, is that Hannah Montana?"

Lilly turned and saw Hannah pushing her way through the crowd.

"Hey, everybody!" Miley called out. "I'm just here to wish my number-one fan happy birthday. But don't mind me—the whole day is about Lilly!"

When Miley finally reached her friend, she whispered, "I didn't have a choice! I swear I'll make it up to you."

"You will never, ever, *ever* be able to make it up to me," Lilly said.

Lilly turned and started walking away. She couldn't believe her so-called best friend would do this to her!

Oswald rushed up to her. "Is it true that Hannah grew up in a notable neighborhood in Nashville?"

"More like a cornfield in Crowley Corners," Lilly muttered, glaring at Miley, who was surrounded by a crowd of fans.

The next day, Mr. Stewart was still furious. He couldn't believe Miley had forgotten to say good-bye to Jackson. Or that she'd shown up at Lilly's party dressed as Hannah Montana. Or that she'd agreed to do the New York Music Awards without checking with him first.

"New York's not happening," he told Vita. "We're flying to Tennessee for Grandma Ruby's birthday."

He started off down the beach to find Miley. She was trying to call Lilly on her cell phone, but Lilly wouldn't answer.

"I know I screwed up," Miley told her dad. "I'm sorry. But I can't talk about this now. I have to go to New York."

"So your grandma's birthday doesn't even—" Mr. Stewart began.

"*Daaaaad!*" Miley whined. "This is different."

"Yeah," Mr. Stewart replied. "In the grand scheme of life, one of these things is actually important."

"Hannah not going really isn't an option," Vita chimed in. "We'll get her a private jet if we have to."

"Yes!" Miley exclaimed. "I always wanted one of those!"

For a second, Mr. Stewart was ready to explode. What had happened to Miley? Since when did she care so much about designer clothes, award shows, and private planes? Then he had an idea.

"Fine," he told Vita. "You win. But you heard our superstar. She wants a jet."

Later, on the private plane, Miley squeezed through a narrow restroom door. She was struggling with the Hannah Box. "Next time you might want to demand a jet with a bigger bathroom," she complained to her father. Vita had gone on ahead to New York to arrange things. It was just the two of them on the plane.

"Why you getting all Hannah'd up?" Mr. Stewart asked, observing her stylish clothes and makeup.

"The Hannah-steps-off-the-plane photo op!" Miley answered. "Like Vita says, it's all about the publicity!"

When the jet landed, Miley, dressed as Hannah, was ready to greet her fans. She strode to the door and struck a pose. "Hello, New York!" she cried.

Then she blinked. All she saw was a field, empty except for a few cows.

A pickup truck rattled up, and Jackson beeped the horn. "Looks like your limo's here," Mr. Stewart commented.

"Hannah Montana is supposed to be walking down a red carpet in New York in less than three hours!" Miley cried. She couldn't believe her father had rerouted the plane to Tennessee.

"Miley, all you've ever wanted was to sing," Mr. Stewart said. "Hannah let you do that and still have a normal life. That's why we created her. But I don't know if that's what she's about anymore."

"You can't take Hannah away!" Miley cried. "Hannah means everything to me!"

"And that right there might just be our problem," Mr. Stewart replied.

Miley stared at him. It finally sank in—her father was serious.

"I can never be Hannah again?"

"Ask me in two weeks," Mr. Stewart replied. "Let's see if the country girl still exists."

Suddenly Miley felt the wig being lifted off her head. She spun around and saw a beautiful horse holding the wig in his mouth.

"Give that back!" she cried.

Mr. Stewart shook his head. "Girl doesn't even recognize her own horse."

Miley stared. "Blue Jeans?" she said.

"Why don't we meet you at the house?" Mr. Stewart said. "It's just about a mile up the road. Don't forget your suitcase." He and Jackson drove off, leaving Miley behind.

Miley scrambled onto the horse's back. But when she reached down for her suitcases, she fell off. Blue Jeans took off running across the field.

"Blue Jeans, come back!" Miley yelled.

Suddenly another horse raced past carrying a boy around Miley's age. The boy galloped after Blue Jeans and lassoed her!

He returned slowly, leading Miley's horse.

"You okay?" he asked. The boy stared at her for a minute, then said, "Miley? It's me, Travis Brody."

"I remember you!" she said. Travis had had a crush on her when they were little. Now he was all grown up!

Travis offered Miley a hand, and he pulled her up onto his horse. They rode off toward her grandmother's house, leading Blue Jeans.

"How long are you staying?" Travis asked.

"Two weeks," Miley said with a frown.

"Good luck," Travis said. "I'm guessing you've gone all California on us."

"You don't know anything about me. Or California," Miley retorted.

"Let me guess," Travis teased. "Celebrities are regular folk just like you and me. You actually know any?"

"I know Hannah Montana," Miley blurted out. "We're like best friends."

When they reached Grandma Ruby's farmhouse, Travis left to put the horses in the barn.

Miley went into the house. Her family and many friends were singing and laughing together.

"Hey everybody," Miley said, feeling awkward.

"I just blew out my candles, and I've already got my birthday wish!" Grandma Ruby exclaimed. "Come here, sweet thing."

"Happy birthday, Grandma," Miley said as she gave her grandmother a hug.

Later that night, Miley sat in her bedroom looking at an old photograph of her and her mother.

"I keep thinking that I should change the wallpaper," Grandma Ruby said as she walked into the room. "But your mom picked it out when she was about your age."

"I like it," Miley said.

"You used to like a lot of things about coming to see me." Her grandmother paused. "I just miss my Miley."

"Why do people keep saying that?" Miley asked.

"Maybe you should be asking yourself that question," Grandma Ruby replied. She gave Miley a kiss and walked out of the room.

Miley thought being back in Crowley Corners would be boring compared to her life as Hannah Montana. But over the next couple of days, she discovered some interesting things.

She found out that Jackson hadn't gotten into college after all. He was working at their cousin's petting zoo! Their father didn't know, and Jackson wanted to keep it that way.

Miley also noticed that her father was spending a lot of time with a woman named Lorelai, who worked at the farm. And he seemed . . . happy.

One day she went to the farmer's market in town with her grandma. Once there, Miley noticed a big sign that said SAVE CROWLEY MEADOWS: FUND-RAISER THIS SATURDAY.

"Old Man Crowley died and left the town the Meadows," Grandma Ruby explained. "But we don't have enough for the taxes. It's just awful! Developers circling like vultures, talking about putting up apartment buildings, shopping malls . . ."

Her grandmother pointed out the table where one of the developers, Mr. Bradley, was showing off his model of the new Crowley Corners development. Miley smiled at the thought of a new mall. Then there would finally be something fun to do.

Grandma Ruby nodded toward a shoe store. The window showed a bunch of dusty, out-of-style shoes.

"When we're finished, maybe you and I can do a little shopping," she said.

"In there? No thanks." Miley grimaced. She wouldn't be

caught dead wearing any of those shoes.

Grandma Ruby frowned. "Look, missy. You might be fooling your daddy, but you sure as heck ain't fooling me!"

Miley felt a flash of guilt. Was she really acting that snobby?

Her grandma's face softened. "You should consider yourself lucky that for the time being you have a place like this to call home."

"I'm sorry," Miley said.

She looked around at the small town center and open fields.

Was she lucky to have this place?

Suddenly Miley heard a familiar voice. "Excuse me. Do you know this girl?"

She whirled around. It was Oswald Granger! He was showing a woman a photo of Hannah Montana. How had he found her *here*?

Miley had to distract him! She dumped a truckload of walnuts in his path. They made him stumble and fall—right on top of the model of Crowley Meadows!

"Miley, help me with this poor man," Grandma Ruby called as she pulled Oswald to his feet.

"You're too kind, really," Oswald muttered. His eyes lit up when he saw Miley. "Hey, do you know this Hannah Montana?"

Miley quickly explained that the Montanas lived a few miles out of town. Grandma Ruby caught on quickly, and together, they gave Oswald some made-up directions.

Oswald looked confused. But he pulled out a map and limped away.

Miley and Grandma Ruby rushed home to tell Mr. Stewart what had happened. He assured them that Oswald probably didn't know anything about their secret.

Miley went out to the barn with her guitar, to get away from her problems for a while.

She started to play and sing. After a minute, she noticed she wasn't alone. Travis was there, listening!

"Sorry," he said as she stopped abruptly. "Don't stop."

"I'm just goofing around," Miley said.

Travis smiled. "I think it's great you're still doing that singing thing. Everybody knows that's all you ever wanted to do."

She asked what he thought of her song.

"It sounded like you got most of the notes right," he said. "It just wasn't . . . *about* anything. It didn't tell me who you are. What you feel." He smiled sheepishly. "Sorry."

He went back to work repairing Grandma Ruby's old chicken coop. Miley watched for a moment.

"Why are you even bothering with that?" she asked.

Travis explained that he wanted to start an egg business. Her grandmother had told him that if he fixed the coop, he could sell the eggs.

"So that's all you want to do?" Miley asked. "Sell eggs in Crowley Corners?"

"You just don't get this place at all, do you? Come on. Let's go." He grabbed Miley's hand.

Before she knew it, Miley was riding Blue Jeans alongside Travis and his horse. Soon they reached a hidden pond with a waterfall. When she saw it, memories flooded Miley's mind.

"This is our place!" she cried. "I forgot it was even real!"

She and Travis spent the afternoon swimming and having a good time. It was actually the most fun Miley could remember having in a while.

Suddenly, everything about life on the farm seemed more interesting.

Maybe her father had the right idea. Sure, being Hannah Montana was great, but so was being plain old Miley Stewart.

When the day of the fund-raiser rolled around, the townspeople gathered at a local club for Open Mic Night. Mr. Stewart had a great time singing with a local band. When he finished, he went outside for some fresh air with Lorelai. But Miley hardly noticed. She and Travis were dancing together. It felt nice. *Really* nice.

When the song ended, Travis looked at Miley. "It's open mic," he said. "Want to give it a try?"

Miley gulped. "I'm good, thanks."

But Travis was already jumping onstage. "Come on up, Miley!"

Miley wasn't sure what to do. If she started to sing, would everyone recognize her voice? Or, rather, *Hannah's* voice?

Then she had an idea. Instead of singing, she started a sort of rap with a country twist. She made up dance moves as she went along.

The townspeople loved it. A few started copying her moves, turning them into a line dance. Before long, everyone was joining in.

When she finished, the crowd cheered.

Miley grinned. It felt good to hear applause again!

But the cheers were quickly interrupted by her grandmother's voice. "You've got a lot of nerve coming in here!"

Everyone froze. Miley glanced over and saw her grandmother glaring at Mr. Bradley.

The developer shrugged. "You ain't never gonna raise the kind of money it's gonna take to save the Meadows."

"Miley knows Hannah Montana!" Travis blurted out. "They're best friends. She could give a concert."

Everyone in the club turned to look at Miley.

The next day, a limo drove into Crowley Corners. It stopped at Grandma Ruby's house.

"She's here!" Miley cried happily. "I didn't know if she'd really come!"

Miley had asked Lilly to put on Hannah's wig and come to Crowley Corners. She hadn't been sure Lilly would play along this time. Not after that disastrous party.

Miley raced out to greet her friend. Lilly climbed out of the limo dressed as Hannah. "Thank you, thank you, thank you," Miley said, hugging her.

"Vita said I could keep the clothes," Lilly replied with a shrug.

Miley and Lilly went up to Miley's room.

"I am so sorry," she said sincerely. "You're the best friend I ever had. When I thought I might lose you forever . . ."

Lilly finally smiled. That was all she'd been waiting for— a *real* apology.

"Hey, you couldn't lose me even if you wanted to!" Lilly said. They hugged.

Just then, Lorelai knocked on the door. She wanted to talk to Hannah!

Lilly was still wearing Hannah's wig. She quickly hid under the covers and pretended to be recovering from jet lag.

Miley went downstairs to tell her dad what was going on. While she was gone, Lilly agreed that Hannah would go to a dinner that night, hosted by the mayor.

Later that afternoon Miley and Lilly saw Travis fixing a fence on the front lawn. Miley explained how she and Travis had grown close lately. But they were still just friends. Then she had an idea. "He hasn't met Hannah yet . . ."

Miley stepped onto the porch dressed as Hannah Montana. Travis was still focused on his work.

"Oh, hi," Travis said when he looked up. "I'm Travis. Thanks for coming. Welcome to Crowley Corners."

Miley was surprised that Travis didn't seem all that interested in her.

"So you and Miley are pretty close?" he asked. "Do you think she'd go out with me if I asked?"

Miley couldn't believe it. He *did* like her as more than friends! "What are you telling me all this for? Go ask her out!"

Then she remembered: he couldn't. Not while she was standing there dressed as Hannah. She told him Miley was out in the barn while she raced inside to change.

But when Travis couldn't find Miley outside, he tried the house. Lilly and Grandma Ruby were shelling peas on the porch and directed him into the kitchen. Miley, now back to her real self, had to climb down the trellis to avoid him! Soon she was outside by the chicken coop, where he finally found her.

"I was just talking to your friend Hannah," he said shyly. "We were talking about you . . . I was wondering . . . would you like to go to dinner with me this evening?"

Miley smiled. "Sure," she said. "I don't think I have any plans."

But later when she told her father, he reminded her that Hannah was supposed to go to the mayor's dinner that night.

"I'll leave it up to you," Mr. Stewart said. "Do whatever you think is right."

That evening Miley rode to the town hall dressed as Hannah with her dad and Lilly. Travis was waiting for her in a restaurant right across the street.

When everyone was seated, the mayor began a long, rambling speech welcoming Hannah to town.

Miley barely heard it. She was staring out the window at the restaurant.

Suddenly, Miley blurted out, "I really need to use the bathroom."

She grabbed Lilly and they raced into the hall. Lilly had hidden the Hannah Box in a broom closet. Miley ducked inside and changed into her regular clothes. Then she dashed across the street to meet Travis.

"Sorry I'm late!" Miley said as she slid into her chair.

"You're not late, I was early," Travis said. He paused, then continued, "Miley, I want to make sure you know how I feel about you."

Just then Miley's cell phone rang.

"I should take this," she said, jumping to her feet. "I'll get better reception in back."

For the rest of the night, Miley kept busy running back and forth between the town hall and the restaurant. It wasn't easy to keep coming up with excuses to leave either place. She had to convince Jackson to tell college stories to distract everyone from Hannah's disappearances.

Finally, as Miley tried to leave the mayor's dinner again, her father exploded.

"Sit!" he thundered. "No one is getting up from this table!"

Mr. Stewart turned to Jackson. "No more stories about a university you don't even attend!"

Jackson looked stunned. "You knew?"

It turned out Mr. Stewart had known all along. It had been his idea to make Jackson work at the petting zoo!

Jackson had brought a ferret to the dinner. It had just escaped and crawled up the mayor's leg. The mayor leaped to his feet and yelled!

In the chaos that followed, Miley ran out again. When she reached the broom closet, a cleaning lady was there. She grabbed her box and sprinted off, looking for another place to change.

She decided on the town hall's revolving door. But when she came out, she found Travis staring at her. He'd seen her transformation!

"Let me explain!" Miley blurted out.

"Explain what?" Travis looked angry. "How you've been lying to me this whole time? I never would have treated you this way."

Miley watched, heartbroken, as Travis stomped away.

The next day, Miley sat under the gazebo on Grandma Ruby's farm strumming her guitar.

"Hey," her father said as he approached. He sat down next to her.

"You mad?" Miley asked him.

"Nah," Mr. Stewart replied. "How's the song coming?"

Miley wasn't sure. But she played it for him. It was all about her life and her dad. When she finished, Mr. Stewart smiled proudly.

"It's good, Miley," he said.

Miley was glad she and her father were back on track. But she wondered whether she'd ever get the rest of her life straightened out.

The next day was Hannah's concert for the Save Crowley Meadows event. She took the stage and started singing. But partway through the song, she spotted Travis in the crowd. She tried to keep singing. But her heart wasn't in it.

"I'm sorry," she said into the microphone. The crowd stared at her in silence. "I've loved being Hannah. But I don't think I can do it anymore. At least not here. This is family." She pulled off her wig. The crowd gasped. "Hi. It's me. I've hurt a lot of people, but I didn't mean to." She stared straight at Travis. "If it's not too late, I sure would like a second chance."

Then Miley started singing another song. It was the one she'd written herself that past week.

"Thanks for letting me live my Hannah," she said to the audience when she finished. "Bye."

She started to walk offstage. But a young fan called out to her. "Please be Hannah!" the little girl begged. "We'll keep your secret."

"It's too late," Miley said. "I can't. . . ."

"Sure you can!" Travis called out.

Miley couldn't believe it. Travis *wanted* her to be Hannah?

Everyone else promised to keep her secret, too. Well, all except one person . . .

"I got the story," Oswald was saying into his cell phone. "Photos and all!"

"Don't do it, man!" Mr. Stewart cried.

"Sorry," Oswald said. "There's nothing on earth that could stop me from—"

"Daddy! Daddy!" Two young girls with British accents raced over. Vita had flown Oswald's daughters over from England to meet their idol, Hannah Montana.

"Are you really going to destroy their dreams?" Vita whispered to Oswald. "Because that's what Hannah is all about."

Looking at his daughters' excited faces was enough to convince Oswald to keep Miley's secret. He quit his job, then hung up on his editor without telling her anything.

Vita smiled. "Let's go," she said to Miley. "Something tells me Hannah has a few more songs in her."

Travis grabbed Miley's hand.

"What do you say?" he said. "Ready to get back up there and have some fun?"

"I say, I think you still have a crush on me!" she said with a grin.

He laughed. Then he leaned in and kissed her—finally. She kissed him back. She'd been waiting for that kiss for days! When the kiss ended, she smiled at him and then hurried off to give her fans another song.

She was back to living her dream. And now she understood that she really did have the best of both worlds.

THE END